This Little Tiger book
belongs to:

_____

_____

_____

For anyone who has ever been held captive by a book
~ J K

For two Australian princesses, Mia and Ava
~ E E

LITTLE TIGER PRESS LTD,
an imprint of the Little Tiger Group
1 Coda Studios, 189 Munster Road,
London SW6 6AW
www.littletiger.co.uk

First published in Great Britain 2019
This edition published 2020

Printed in China · LTP/1400/2944/1019
2 4 6 8 10 9 7 5 3 1

SHHH!
I'M READING!

JOHN KELLY • ELINA ELLIS

LITTLE TiGER

LONDON

It was a wet and windy Sunday afternoon, but Bella didn't care. She was busy reading the best book EVER! And the story had just reached the AMAZING bit, right near the end where . . .

"AHOY, Shipmate Bella!" bellowed Captain Bluebottom the Flatulent. "It's Sunday! Are you ready for another adventure with the Windy Pirates?"

"Sorry, Captain," said Bella,
"but today I'd rather just sit
and read my book."

"READ A BOOK?" harrumphed Bluebottom.
"BY MY WINDY TROUSERS! How could a book
be better than a voyage to Devil's Island, a duel with
Nobby the Nasty,

and then home again with a ship full of booty?

AAARGHHH!"

"Well, this book is!" said Bella.
"So you can all drop anchor
and sit quietly because
I AM BUSY READING!"

Bella picked up her book
and began to read the
AMAZING bit, right near
the end where . . .

"Bella, darling," squawked Maurice Penguin.
"Why aren't you ready? It's Sunday afternoon!
It's SHOWTIME!"

"Not now!" said Bella. "I'd really rather sit and read my book."

"READ A BOOK?" cried Maurice. "How could a book be more fabulous than the tippity-tap-tap of your shoes on stage, the roar of applause, and this **SPANGLY** costume?"

"WOW!" said Bella. "But this book is even more fabulous than ALL those sequins!" She pointed to the band. "EVERYONE TAKE FIVE! And please be quiet, **I AM BUSY READING!**"

Bella picked up her book and
turned to the AMAZING bit
near the end where . . .

"I claim this bedroom in the name of the Lardon Empire!" announced Emperor Flabulon the Wobbulous. "NOT NOW!" exclaimed Bella. "I'm reading this BOOK!"

"But it's Sunday!" burbled Flabulon. "You always defend the Earth on a Sunday afternoon."

"I know," sighed Bella. "But today **I AM BUSY READING!**"

"READING?" splurted Flabulon.

"How could a book be more exciting than blazing laser cannons, dodging anti-matter missiles, and zooming dangerously fast in a really cool **SPACESHIP?**

"WELL, THIS BOOK IS!" said Bella.
"Look, I'll save the Earth after teatime!
Plop your tentacles in the corner and
BE QUIET! For the last time,
I AM BUSY READING!"

At long last there was peace and quiet.

Bella read on until, just before teatime,
she reached the end of her book.

"That was the BEST BOOK EVER!"
she announced. "Now, who wants to go on
an INCREDIBLE adventure?"

Everyone looked up at her and said . . .

"Maybe later, Bella,
but right now . . .

WE ARE BUSY
READING!"

SHHH!

We're reading more magical stories from Little Tiger Press!

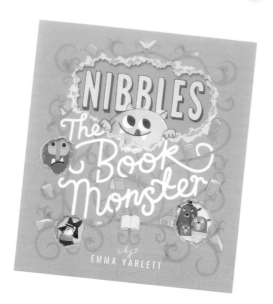

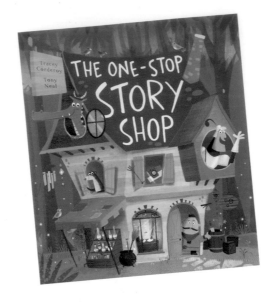

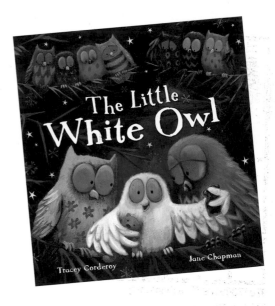

For information regarding any of the above titles or for our catalogue, please contact us:
Little Tiger Press Ltd, 1 Coda Studios, 189 Munster Road, London SW6 6AW
Tel: 020 7385 6333 · E-mail: contact@littletiger.co.uk · www.littletiger.co.uk